On Sudden Hill

*For Stephen – **LS***

*For Auntie Jan and summers spent
painting at Pondok – **BD***

SIMON AND SCHUSTER
First published in Great Britain in 2014 by Simon and Schuster UK Ltd, 1st Floor, 222 Gray's Inn Road, London WC1X 8HB
A CBS Company • Text copyright © Linda Sarah 2014 • Illustration copyright © Benji Davies 2014 • The right of Linda Sarah
and Benji Davies to be identified as the author and illustrator of this work has been asserted by them in accordance with
the Copyright, Designs and Patents Act, 1988 • All rights reserved, including the right of reproduction in whole or in part
in any form • A CIP catalogue record for this book is available from the British Library upon request • Printed in China
ISBN: 978-1-4711-1928-6 (HB) • ISBN: 978-1-47114-506-3 (PB) • ISBN: 978-1-4711-1930-9 (eBook) • 10 9 8 7 6 5 4 3 2 1

On Sudden Hill

Linda Sarah and Benji Davies

SIMON AND SCHUSTER
London   New York   Sydney   Toronto   New Delhi

Two cardboard boxes,
big enough to sit in, hide inside.

Birt and Etho take them out each day,
climb up Sudden Hill and sit in them.

Sometimes they're kings,
soldiers, astronauts.
Sometimes they're pirates
sailing wild seas and skies.

But always, always
they're Big friends.

Their sailing, running, leaping, flying,
their chatter and giggles,
him and Etho,

their silences
and watching small movements
in the valley and feeling
big as Giant Kings.

Birt loves their two-by-two rhythm.

And then one Monday
(it's cramping cold)
they meet another box-carrier
who wants to join them.

    This tiny boy's called Shu.
    He's watched Birt and Etho every day
    and finally found a big enough box
    and courage to ask if he can play too.

Etho smiles and says, "Sure!"
And so the three sit in their boxes,
watch one kestrel
and two lost clouds.

Sometimes they're dragon-slayers,
side-by-side house dwellers
and skyscraper dancers.

But Birt feels strange.

One night,
Birt smashes his box,
stamps on it,
rips it to bits.

His dad shouts something flat from the front room
about being quiet and that's enough!

Birt stops going up Sudden Hill.

Etho and Shu
call round sometimes.
Birt avoids them.

Instead he stays at home
mostly drawing pictures
of two boxes, side-by-side.

But he misses Etho.
He misses their cardboard
castles on Sudden Hill.

One day,
a knock on the door.

He hears Shu's voice.
"We made you something.
Please come out!"

All Birt can see
as he peeks
from the curtain
is a box.

But it's much,
much more
than a box.

It's got bright, waving things
attached to it like huge kites.
It's got colours.
It's got sound.
It's got, it's got – WHEELS!

The HUGE box-on-wheels
(that they call Mr ClimbFierce)
is hauled up Sudden Hill.

It's amazing!

An incredible Monster Creature Box Thing!

It's a supersonic rocket blaster!
A triple jet transformer!
A sparkling glitter king!

It's even got boxes inside,
one with biscuits, one with lemonade.

Birt likes Shu.
Shu is kind.
Shu is funny.
Shu is daring and brave.

Birt loves their time together,
their Etho-Shu-Birt-iness.

He loves their three-by-three rhythm.

It's new.
And it's good.

This TWO HOOTS book belongs to

_ _ _ _ _ _ _ _ _ _ _ _

Chris, Jim and my
whole family,
I couldn't have done
it without you.

First published 2016 by Two Hoots
This edition published 2017 by Two Hoots
an imprint of Pan Macmillan
20 New Wharf Road, London N1 9RR
Associated companies throughout the world
www.panmacmillan.com
ISBN: 978-1-4472-9140-4
Text and illustrations © Bethan Woollvin 2016
Moral rights asserted.

3 5 7 9 8 6 4 2
A CIP catalogue record for this book is available from the British Library.
Printed in China
The illustrations in this book were painted in gouache on cartridge paper.

www.twohootsbooks.com

Little Red

Bethan Woollvin

TW🐦 HOOTS

One day, Little Red Riding Hood's mother called to her.

"Please take some cake to your Grandma," she said.
"She's not feeling too well."

So Little Red Riding Hood set off
on her journey through the forest
to Grandma's house.

Before long, she met a wolf.

"Where are you going?" he growled.

Which might have scared some little girls.

But not this little girl.

"To my Grandma's," Little Red replied.

"She's not feeling well."

"Is that right?" said the wolf.

And he made a plan.

The wolf said goodbye to
Little Red Riding Hood, took a shortcut through
the trees, and found Grandma's house.

Which was unlucky for Grandma.

He put on her glasses and spare nightdress,
and climbed into Grandma's bed.

And there he waited.

It wasn't long before Little Red arrived
and found the door to Grandma's house
was already open. She peeped in
through the window.

Inside she couldn't see Grandma,
but she could see a badly disguised
wolf waiting in Grandma's bed!

Which might have scared
some little girls.
But not this little girl.

She made a plan,
and went inside.

"Hello Grandma," Little Red Riding Hood said and, though she wasn't fooled for a minute, she played along with the wolf's disguise.

"Oh Grandma! What big ears you have!" she said.

"Oh Grandma! What big eyes you have!" she said.

And, "Oh Grandma! What big TEETH you have!" she said.

"Why yes, my dear," replied the wolf.
"All the better to . . ."

EAT YOU WITH!

And the wolf leapt forwards.

Which might have scared
some little girls . . .

. . . but not this little girl.

Which was unlucky for the wolf.

From the Author

Bethan Woollvin

I created *Little Red* as part of my illustration
course at University, and it won me The Macmillan
Prize for Illustration. As a child I found Little
Red Riding Hood very naive: how could she not
tell it was a wolf in a nightdress? I wanted my
Little Red to be braver and more intelligent
than the original! Above all I wanted to make
something that my family would enjoy –
I'm the oldest of ten children and I love
reading stories to my brothers and
sisters. They really like *Little Red*
and I hope you do too.